THE
WIZARD
OF
OZ

Published by Simon & Schuster, Inc.
Copyright © 1985 by Simon & Schuster, Inc.
Illustrations copyright © 1985 by Dennis Hockerman
All rights reserved
including the right of reproduction
in whole or in part in any form.
Published by LITTLE SIMON,
a Division of Simon & Schuster, Inc.,
Simon & Schuster Building,
Rockefeller Center,
1230 Avenue of the Americas,
New York, New York 10020.
LITTLE SIMON and colophon are trademarks of Simon & Schuster, Inc.
Manufactured in the United States of America.
10 9 8 7 6 5 4 3 2 1

Library of Congress Cataloging in Publication Data

Baum, L. Frank (Lyman Frank), 1856–1919.
The Wizard of Oz.
Summary: After being transported by a cyclone
to the land of Oz, Dorothy and her dog are befriended
by a scarecrow, a tin man, and a cowardly lion,
who accompany her to the Emerald City to look for
a wizard who can help Dorothy return home to Kansas.
[1. Fantasy] I. Hockerman, Dennis, ill.
II. Title.
PZ7.B327Wi   1985b   [E]   85-14824

ISBN: 0-671-60504-6

THE WIZARD OF OZ

Adapted from the story by
L. FRANK BAUM

Illustrated by Dennis Hockerman

Little Simon
Published by Simon & Schuster, Inc., New York

Dorothy lived in the midst of the great Kansas prairies, with Uncle Henry, who was a farmer, and Aunt Em, his wife. Their house was small, for the lumber to build it had to be carried by wagon many miles.

When Dorothy stood in the doorway and looked around, she could see nothing but the great, gray prairie on every side. Long ago the house had been painted, but the sun blistered the paint and the rains washed it away, and now it was as dull and gray as everything else.

The sun and wind had changed Aunt Em and Uncle Henry, too. A life of hard work had robbed the sparkle from their eyes and the rosiness from their cheeks, and they also were gray.

Were it not for Toto, Dorothy too would have grown as colorless as her surroundings. Toto was a little black dog with long, silky hair and small, black eyes that twinkled merrily on either side of his funny, wee nose. Toto and Dorothy played together all day long.

Today, however, they were not playing. Uncle Henry sat on the steps and looked anxiously at the sky. Dorothy stood in the doorway with Toto in her arms and looked at the sky, too. From the far north they heard the low wail of the wind, and Uncle Henry and Dorothy could see where the long grass bowed in waves before the coming storm.

Suddenly Uncle Henry stood up.

"There's a cyclone coming, Em," he called to his wife. "I'll go look after the animals."

Aunt Em came to the door. One glance told her of the danger close at hand.

"Quick, Dorothy!" she shouted. "Run for the cellar!"

Just as Aunt Em threw open the trapdoor and started to climb down the ladder into the small, dark hole, Toto jumped out of Dorothy's arms, ran inside, and hid under Dorothy's bed. Dorothy caught Toto at last and started to run after her aunt. But when she was almost to the door, there came a great shriek from the wind, and the house shook so hard that she lost her footing and fell to the floor.

Then a strange thing happened. The house whirled around two or three times and rose slowly through the air. The great pressure of the wind on every side of the house raised it up higher and higher, until it was at the very top of the cyclone. There it remained and was carried miles and miles away, as easily as you could carry a feather.

To her amazement, she saw that the cyclone had set the house down in the midst of a country of marvelous beauty. As she gazed at the beautiful sights, she noticed that coming toward her was a group of the most peculiar-looking people she had ever seen. There were three men and one old woman. All were even smaller than Dorothy and each wore a round hat that rose to a small point a foot above their heads, with little bells around the brims that tinkled sweetly as they moved.

"You are welcome, most noble sorceress, to the land of the Munch-kins," said the old woman. "We are so grateful to you for having killed the Wicked Witch of the East, and for setting our countrymen free."

"There must be some mistake," answered Dorothy. "I've never killed anything in my life."

"Your house did, anyway," replied the little old woman. "Look!" And she pointed to the corner of the house.

"Oh, dear! Oh, dear!" cried Dorothy. There indeed, just out from under the corner of the house, stuck two feet that were shod in silver shoes with pointed toes.

"She was the Wicked Witch of the East," explained the woman. "The Munchkins have been her slaves for many years. Now they are all set free, thanks to you."

"Who are the Munchkins?" inquired Dorothy.

"They are the people who live in this Land of the East, where the Wicked Witch ruled."

"Are you a Munchkin?" asked Dorothy.

"No, though I am their friend. I am the Witch of the North."

"Oh, gracious!" cried Dorothy. "Are you a *real* witch?"

"Yes, indeed. But I am a Good Witch. You see, there were only four Witches in all the Land of Oz. Those who dwelt in the East and the West were Wicked Witches, and now you have killed one of them. For your reward," said the old woman as she stopped by the Wicked Witch's feet, "you may have her silver shoes."

"There was some charm connected to them," said one of the Munchkins, "but what it was, we never knew."

Dorothy took off her worn leather shoes and tried on the silver ones. They fitted her as well as if they had been made for her. Beautiful though they were, Dorothy had but one thought on her mind. "I am anxious to get back to my aunt and uncle who live in Kansas, for I am sure they will worry about me. Can you help me find my way?" she asked the Witch of the North.

The old woman thought for a time. Then she said, "I do not know where Kansas is, for I have never heard that country mentioned before. But a great desert surrounds this land, and no one has ever lived to cross it. I'm afraid, my dear, you'll have to live with us."

At this, Dorothy began to sob, for she felt lonely among all these strange people. Her tears seemed to grieve the kindhearted Munchkins, for they immediately took out their handkerchiefs and began to weep as well.

"Perhaps Oz, the Great Wizard who lives in the City of Emeralds, can help you," said the Good Witch.

"How can I get there?" asked Dorothy.

"You must walk. It is a long journey through a country that is sometimes pleasant but sometimes dark and terrible."

"Won't you go with me?" pleaded Dorothy.

"No, I cannot do that," she replied, "but I will give you a kiss. No one will dare injure a person who has been kissed by the Witch of the North." So saying, the old woman pressed her lips gently to the child's forehead, leaving a round, shining mark to protect Dorothy from harm. "The road to the Emerald City is paved with yellow brick so you cannot miss it. Good-bye, my dear." The Witch gave Dorothy a friendly nod, whirled around on her left heel, and disappeared—much to the surprise of Toto, who barked loudly after her.

"Come along, Toto," Dorothy said. "We will go to the Emerald City and ask the Great Oz how to get back to Kansas." It did not take them long to find the road paved with yellow brick. As she walked along, Dorothy was surprised to see how pretty the country was around her. There were neat fences at the sides of the road and beyond them were fields of grain and vegetables.

When she had gone several miles, she thought she would stop to rest, and so she climbed to the top of the fence beside the road and sat down. There was a great cornfield beyond the fence, and not far away she saw a Scarecrow placed high on a pole to keep the birds from the ripe corn.

While Dorothy was staring at the painted face of the Scarecrow, she was surprised to see one of the black eyes wink at her.

"Good day," said the Scarecrow, in a rather husky voice.

"Did you speak?" asked the girl, in wonder.

"Certainly," answered the Scarecrow.

"Then how do you do?" replied Dorothy politely.

"Not very well," said the Scarecrow. "It is very tedious being perched up here day and night."

"Can't you get down?" asked Dorothy.

"No, this pole is stuck up my back. I should be greatly obliged if you could help me."

Dorothy reached up and lifted the figure off the pole. Being stuffed with straw, he was quite light.

"Thank you very much," said the Scarecrow. "I feel like a new man. By the way, who are you?"

"My name is Dorothy, and I am going to the Emerald City to ask the Great Oz to send me back to Kansas."

"Where is the Emerald City?" asked the Scarecrow.

"Why, don't you know?" she returned in surprise.

"No, I don't know anything at all. You see, I am stuffed, so I have no brains," he answered sadly. "Do you think that if I go to the Emerald City with you, the Great Oz would give me some brains?"

"It couldn't hurt to ask," answered Dorothy, "and I would greatly appreciate the company."

"Thank you," he answered gratefully.

They walked back to the road. Dorothy helped the Scarecrow over the fence, and they started along the path of yellow brick for the great Emerald City.

After a few hours of walking, Dorothy and the Scarecrow sat down by the roadside to rest. Dorothy talked about Kansas and about how much she missed her Aunt Em and Uncle Henry. Just when they were about to go back to the yellow brick road, they were startled to hear a deep groan nearby.

W hat was that?" they whispered at exactly the same time. They turned and walked through the forest a few steps, when Dorothy discovered something gleaming in a ray of sunshine that fell between the trees. She ran to the place and then stopped short. One of the big trees had been partly chopped through. Standing beside it, with an uplifted ax in his hands, was a man made entirely of tin. He stood perfectly still, as if he couldn't move at all.

"Did you groan?" asked Dorothy.

"Yes," answered the Tin Woodman. "I did. Would you get an oilcan and oil my joints? They are rusted so badly that I cannot move them an inch."

The Tin Woodman's cottage was nearby. In it, Dorothy found an oilcan. Then she carefully oiled all the Tin Woodman's joints until they were quite free from rust and as good as new.

The Tin Woodman gave a sigh of relief and lowered his ax. "I might have stood there forever if you had not come along," he said. "You have saved my life. How did you happen to be here?"

"We are on our way to the Emerald City to see the Great Oz," answered Dorothy. "I want him to send me back to Kansas, and the Scarecrow wants him to put a few brains in his head."

"Do you suppose Oz could give me a heart? I would give anything to have one," said the Tin Woodman earnestly.

"Why don't you ask him yourself?" replied Dorothy.

"Yes, come along with us," said the Scarecrow heartily.

So the Tin Woodman joined them on their journey over the yellow brick road to the Emerald City. After they had walked for some time, they found themselves in a thick, dark wood. The road was still paved with yellow bricks, but many of them were covered with dead leaves, and the walking was difficult.

"How long will it be," Dorothy asked of the Tin Woodman, "before we are out of the forest?"

"I cannot tell," he answered.

J ust as he spoke, there came from the forest a terrible roar. The next moment, a great Lion bounded into the road. Little Toto, now that he had an enemy to face, ran barking toward the Lion, and the great beast opened his mouth to bite the dog. Dorothy, fearing Toto would be killed, rushed toward him without thinking of her own safety. She slapped the Lion upon his nose as hard as she could, and cried out, "Don't you dare bite Toto! You ought to be ashamed of yourself, a big beast like you, picking on such a little dog!"

"I didn't bite him," whimpered the Lion, rubbing his nose with his great paw.

"No, but you tried to," she retorted. "You are nothing but a big coward! That's what you are."

"I know it," said the Lion, hanging his head in shame.

"But the King of Beasts shouldn't be a coward," said the Scarecrow.

"I know," answered the Lion, wiping a tear from his eye with the tip of his tail. "It is my great sorrow. But how can I help it?"

"You could ask the Great Oz to help you," said the Tin Woodman.

"Do you think he could give me courage?" said the Cowardly Lion, his face brightening.

"Just as easily as he could give me brains," said the Scarecrow.

"Or give me a heart," said the Tin Woodman.

"Or send me back to Kansas," said Dorothy.

"Then if you don't mind, I'll go with you," said the Lion, "for my life is simply unbearable without a bit of courage."

Once more the little company set off upon their journey. On and on they walked until finally Dorothy noticed a beautiful, green glow in the sky just before them.

"That must be the Emerald City," said Dorothy.

They quickened their pace, and all the while the emerald green glow grew brighter and brighter until they arrived at the end of the road.

There stood a big gate, all studded with emeralds that glittered in the sun. Beside the gate was a bell. Dorothy rang the bell and the big gate swung open. The travelers found themselves in a high, arched room, the walls of which glistened with countless emeralds. Before them stood a little man with green whiskers.

"What do you wish in the Emerald City?" he asked.

"We came to see the Great Oz," said Dorothy.

"Oh, my," said the little man, shaking his head in perplexity. "If you have come on an idle or foolish errand to bother the Great Oz . . ."

But Dorothy quickly assured him that she and her companions were desperately in need of the Wizard's help.

"Then I will take you to his palace," said the man. "But first you must put on spectacles, or the glory of the Emerald City will blind you."

He opened a box beside him and found spectacles to fit each one of them. Then they all followed him through the portals into the streets of the Emerald City.

Even with eyes protected by the green spectacles, Dorothy and her friends were at first dazzled by the brilliance of Oz. The streets were lined with houses all built of green marble and studded everywhere with sparkling emeralds.

There were many people walking about, and all were dressed in green. The Guardian of the Gate led them through the streets until they came to a big building standing exactly in the middle of the city. There the Guardian took his leave.

"You have come to the Palace of Oz," said a soldier in a green uniform, who was guarding the building. "Step inside."

He led them into a big room with a green carpet and lovely green furniture set with emeralds.

"Please make yourselves comfortable while I tell the Great Oz that you are here."

After a long wait, Dorothy heard a bell ring. Then a girl in a green silk gown, with green hair and green eyes, appeared and said to Dorothy, "That is the signal. You must enter the Throne Room alone."

Dorothy opened a little door and walked boldly into a round room with a high, arched roof. The walls, ceilings, and floor were covered with emeralds. But what interested Dorothy the most was the big throne of green marble that stood in the middle of the room; hovering above the center of the chair was an enormous head. There was no hair upon this head, but it had eyes, a nose, and a mouth, and was bigger than the head of the biggest giant.

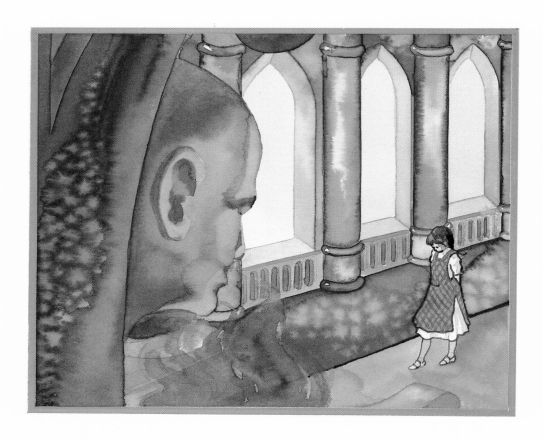

As Dorothy gazed upon this in wonder and fear, the eyes turned slowly and looked at her. Then the mouth moved and she heard a voice say, "I am Oz, the Great and Terrible. Who are you, and why do you seek me?"

"I am Dorothy, the Small and Meek," she answered, "and I have come to you for help."

"What do you wish me to do?" asked the Wizard.

"Send me back to Kansas, where my Aunt Em and Uncle Henry are," she answered.

"I will give you my answer," said Oz. "If you wish me to use my magic power to send you home again, you must do something for me first."

"What must I do?" asked the girl.

"Kill the Wicked Witch of the West," answered Oz. "I see by your silver shoes that you have already killed one witch."

"I didn't kill her willingly," sobbed Dorothy.

"You must kill the Witch of the West," repeated Oz. "Now go, and do not come back until you have completed your task."

Sorrowfully, Dorothy left the Throne Room and went back to where the Lion, the Scarecrow, and the Tin Woodman were waiting to hear what Oz had said to her.

One by one, Dorothy's companions were led into the Throne Room to make their requests. And the Terrible Wizard's answer was always the same: Only when the Wicked Witch of the West was dead would Oz grant each special wish.

So the next morning, Dorothy and Toto, the Scarecrow, the Tin Woodman, and the Cowardly Lion set out walking toward the West to find the Wicked Witch.

Now the Wicked Witch's eyes were as powerful as a telescope and could see everywhere. As she stood in the doorway of her castle, she happened to see Dorothy and her friends. They were a long distance off yet, but the Wicked Witch was angry to find them in her country.

It didn't take her long to decide what to do. There was in her cupboard a golden cap, and whosoever owned it could call upon the Winged Monkeys, who would obey any order they were given.

The Witch placed the golden cap on her head and said the magic words, "Ep-pe, pep-pe, kak-ke!" The charm began to work: the sky darkened and the sound of rushing wings filled the air. In a matter of moments, the Wicked Witch was surrounded by a crowd of monkeys, each with a pair of powerful wings on its shoulders.

"Go to the strangers who are within my borders and bring them back to me at once," shrieked the Witch.

The monkeys obeyed her instantly, and once again the sun was clouded over by a multitude of wings. Before long they returned, clutching the frightened travelers in their hairy arms.

The Wicked Witch looked Dorothy over carefully, and when she spied the mark on the girl's forehead, she knew that she dare not hurt the child in any way. She grew even more worried when she saw the silver shoes on Dorothy's feet. But then she happened to look into the child's eyes, and she realized at once that Dorothy did not know how to use the power that the magical shoes bestowed.

"Come with me," snarled the Witch, "and see that you do everything I say, or I will put an end to you. From now on, you and your friends are my slaves!"

And so the poor little group was forced to clean and scour the castle from morning till night. Escape was impossible because the castle was constantly guarded by the Yellow Winkies, who were also enslaved by the Wicked Witch.

Now the Wicked Witch of the West had a great longing to possess Dorothy's silver shoes. Dorothy was so proud of them that she never took them off except at night when she took her bath. But the Witch's dread of water kept her away from Dorothy at bathtime.

So great was the Witch's longing for the magic slippers that she at last thought of a trick to help her attain them. She placed an iron bar in the middle of the kitchen floor, and then used her magic to make it invisible. Since Dorothy could not see the bar, she soon stumbled over it. Luckily she wasn't hurt, but one of her shoes came off in the fall. Before she could reach for it to put it back on, the Witch had snatched it up and placed it on her own foot.

"Give me back my shoe!" Dorothy cried angrily.

"I will not," cackled the Witch. "It is my shoe now! And what's more, someday I'll get the other one, too!"

This made Dorothy so mad that she picked up a bucket of water standing nearby and splashed it all over the Witch. The old woman gave a loud cry of fear. Then, as Dorothy stared on in wonder, the Witch began to shrink before her very eyes.

"See what you have done!" she screamed. "In a minute, I shall melt away!" With these words, the Witch fell down in a brown, molten, shapeless mass.

When the Winkies found out that the Wicked Witch was dead, they rejoiced, for now the spell cast over them was broken and they were free at last. As for Dorothy's friends, they too were filled with joy and could not wait to get back to the Palace of Oz to claim their rewards.

nd so they returned to the Emerald City. When they entered the Throne Room, they heard the Wizard's booming voice and saw the great head.

"I am Oz, the Great and Terrible," he bellowed. "Why do you seek me?"

Dorothy and her friends were once again frightened by the Wizard, but Dorothy spoke up nonetheless. "We have come to claim our promise, O Great Oz."

"What promise is that?" asked the voice of Oz.

"You promised to send me back to Kansas when the Wicked Witch was destroyed," said the girl. And then the Lion, the Tin Woodman, and the Scarecrow reminded Oz of the special promises he had made to each of them, too.

"Is the Wicked Witch of the West really destroyed?" asked the voice.

"Yes," Dorothy answered. "I tossed a bucket of water at her and she melted."

"Dear me," said the voice, "how sudden! Come to me tomorrow, for I must have time to think it over."

"You've had plenty of time already," said the Tin Woodman angrily.

"You must keep your promises to us," reminded Dorothy in a scolding tone.

To frighten the Wizard, the Lion gave a loud roar so fierce that it startled Toto. He jumped away from the Lion in alarm and accidently tipped over the screen that stood in the corner. It fell with a large crash and there, just in the spot the screen had hidden, stood a little old man with a bald head and a meek face.

"Who are you?" asked Dorothy.

"I am Oz, the Great and Terrible," said the little man in weak voice.

"I thought Oz was a great head," said Dorothy.

"No, you are wrong," said the man. "I have been making believe."

"But I don't understand," said Dorothy. "How was it that you appeared to us as a great head?"

"That was one of my tricks," answered Oz. Then he sighed and said, "If you look closely you will see that the head is made out of many thicknesses of paper and has a painted face.

"It is hung from the ceiling by a wire," Oz continued. "And being a ventriloquist, I can throw the sound of my voice wherever I wish."

"Really!" said the Scarecrow. "You ought to be ashamed of yourself for being such a humbug."

"I think you are a very bad man," said Dorothy.

"Oh, no, my dear! I'm a very good man, but I'm a very bad Wizard, I must admit."

"Can't you give me brains?" asked the Scarecrow.

"You don't need them. You are learning something every day. Experience is the only thing that brings knowledge."

"That may be true," said the Scarecrow, "but I shall be very unhappy unless I get some brains."

"Very well," said Oz. "Sit down, please. You must excuse me for taking your head off, but I have to do it."

The man unfastened the Scarecrow's head and replaced the straw with a mixture of bran and a great many pins and needles.

When he fastened the Scarecrow's head on his body again, he said to him, "Hereafter you will be a great man, for I have given you a lot of bran-new brains."

"What about my heart?" said the Tin Woodman.

"I shall have to cut a hole in your chest," said the man.

"Do what you will. It won't hurt, since I'm made of tin."

So the old man cut a hole in the Woodman's chest and placed a lovely red heart made entirely of silk in his breast.

"Now for you, Lion, an extra helping of courage." He went to the cupboard, took down a green bottle, poured its contents into a dish, and instructed the Lion to drink it up as soon as possible.

"What is it?" asked the Lion.

"Well," answered Oz, "if it were inside you, it would be courage. Of course, courage is always inside one; so this really cannot be called courage until you have swallowed it."

The Lion drank from the dish until he had emptied it.

"How do you feel now?" asked Oz.

"Full of courage," replied the Lion proudly.

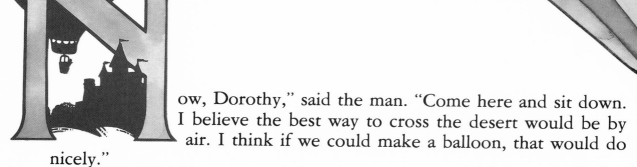

ow, Dorothy," said the man. "Come here and sit down. I believe the best way to cross the desert would be by air. I think if we could make a balloon, that would do nicely."

For three days, Dorothy and Oz worked hard cutting and sewing strips of silk together. At last the balloon was finished, and Oz ordered it carried out in front of the Palace.

All the people in Emerald City gathered around when they saw the balloon. Then Oz got into the basket and announced to all in a loud voice, "I am now going away on a visit. While I am gone, the Scarecrow, the Tin Woodman, and the Lion will rule over you. I command you to obey them as you would me." Suddenly he cried, "Come, Dorothy! Hurry up, or the balloon will fly away!"

At that moment, Toto raced into the crowd to bark at a kitten. Dorothy picked him up and started running toward the balloon. Just when she was within reach of it, *crack!* went the ropes, and the balloon rose into the air without her.

"Come back!" she shouted.

"I can't come back, my dear," called Oz from the basket high overhead. "I don't know how! Good-bye!"

And that was the last any of them ever saw of the Great Wizard. Still, the people of Oz remembered him with loving affection and obeyed their new rulers faithfully.

Dorothy wept bitterly over her lost chance to get to Kansas. In fact, she was crying so hard that she didn't notice the beautiful woman who came floating down from the sky on a radiant sunbeam.

"Please don't cry," said the mysterious stranger. "Is there something I can do for you, my child?"

"Who are you?" said Dorothy through her tears.

"I am Glinda, the Good Witch of the South."

Dorothy told the Witch her whole story—how the cyclone had brought her to the Land of Oz, and how she had come upon many wonderful adventures.

"My greatest wish now," she added, "is to get back to Kansas, for Aunt Em will surely think something dreadful has happened to me."

"Bless your dear heart," said Glinda. "You have had the solution to your problem on your feet all the while. Your silver shoes will carry you over the desert. Had you known of their power, you could have gone back to your Aunt Em the very first day you came to this country."

"But then I would not have had my wonderful brains!" replied the Scarecrow.

"Nor I my lovely heart," said the Tin Woodman.

"And I would have lived a coward forever, " declared the Lion.

"This is all true," said Dorothy, "and I am glad I was of use to these good friends. But now I think I would like to go back to Kansas."

"All you have to do is click the heels of your silver shoes together three times and command the shoes to carry you wherever you wish to go," instructed Glinda, with a smile.

"If that is so," said Dorothy joyfully, "I will ask them to carry me back to Kansas at once."

She threw her arms around the Lion's neck and kissed him, patting his big head tenderly. Then she kissed the Tin Woodman, who was weeping in a way most dangerous to his joints. Last, she hugged the soft, stuffed body of the Scarecrow instead of kissing his painted face, and found she was crying herself at this sorrowful parting from her beloved companions.

Glinda the Good Witch bent down to give the little girl a good-bye kiss, and Dorothy thanked her for her kindness.

Dorothy took Toto up solemnly in her arms and said one last good-bye. Then she clicked the heels of her shoes together three times, saying, "Take me home to Aunt Em!"

Instantly she was whirling through the air, so swiftly that all she could see or feel was the wind whistling past her ears. The silver shoes took but three steps, and then Dorothy stopped so suddenly that she rolled over upon the grass several times before she knew where she was. When she stood up she found she was barefooted, for the silver shoes had fallen off in her flight and were lost forever in the desert.

Just before her was the new farmhouse Uncle Henry had built after the cyclone carried away the old one.

Aunt Em had come out of the house to water the cabbages. When she looked up, she saw Dorothy running toward her.

"My darling child!" she cried, folding the little girl in her arms and covering her face with kisses. "Where in the world did you come from?"

"From the Land of Oz," said Dorothy, gravely. "And here is Toto, too. And oh, Aunt Em! I'm so glad to be back home again!"